Table of Contents

Chapter 1   The Wildlife Refuge............... 2
Chapter 2   The White-Headed Eagles 10
Chapter 3   The Hungry Eaglets 18
Chapter 4   Flying Lessons 26
Chapter 5   Soaring High 32
Chapter 6   Free Again! 38
Glossary 42
Note to Parents and Educators 45
Guidelines for the Young Readers' Series 46

Chapter 1 — The Wildlife Refuge

"Wow!" said Chris. "I've never seen so many trees in my whole life!"

"That's what I thought at first, when I went to camp last summer," said Nikki.

The van went slowly down the long, winding road. Chris and Nikki were on their way to a wildlife refuge.

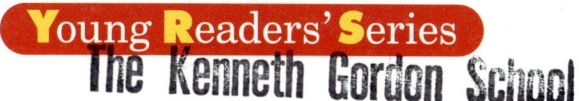
The Kenneth Gordon School

THE BALD EAGLE

Free Again!

Carol A. Amato
Illustrated by Patrick O'Brien

Dedication
With special thanks for her help to
Ms. Deborah Melvin, wildlife biologist with the
U.S. Fish and Wildlife Service

Text © Copyright 1996 by Carol A. Amato
Illustrations © Copyright 1996 by Patrick O'Brien

All rights reserved.
No part of this book may be reproduced in any form by photostat, microfilm, xerography, or any other means, or incorporated into any information retrieval system, electronic or mechanical, without the written permission of the copyright owner.

All inquiries should be addressed to:
Barron's Educational Series, Inc.
250 Wireless Boulevard
Hauppauge, New York 11788

International Standard Book No. 0-8120-9288-0

Library of Congress Catalog Card No. 95-24803
Library of Congress Cataloging-in-Publication Data

Amato, Carol A.
    The bald eagle : free again! / by Carol A. Amato.
        p. cm.—(Young readers' series)
    Summary: On a visit to a wildlife refuge, Chris and Nikki see some bald eagles, both adults and babies, and learn about efforts to protect them.
    ISBN 0-8120-9288-0
    1. Bald eagle—Juvenile literature. 2. Wildlife refuges—Juvenile literature.
  3. Birds, Protection of—Juvenile literature. [1. Bald eagle. 2. Eagles. 3. Endangered species.] I. Title. II. Series: Amato, Carol A. Young readers' series.
    QL696.F32A535   1996
    598.9'16—dc20   95-24803
                                                                        CIP
                                                                         AC

PRINTED IN HONG KONG
6789   9955   987654321

They were learning about endangered animals in their school. The children chose an animal they wanted to learn about. Chris and Nikki chose the bald eagle. Their teacher knew they could find out about the bald eagle at the refuge. She helped them to plan this trip.

"It's just up ahead," said the driver.

"Good," said Chris. "That was a long ride.

The van stopped by a log building. Someone was waiting for them. Nikki and Chris got out of the van.

"Hi!" said the woman who was waiting. "You must be Nikki and Chris."

"Hi!" the children said.

"I hope you'll enjoy your day here. My name is Bess Turner. I'd like you to call me Bess. I'm a wildlife biologist, and I'll be with you today. There are many animals in this refuge."

"What's a refuge?" asked Chris.

"A wildlife refuge is a place where wild animals and plants are protected. This refuge was made to protect bald eagles. I know that you have been learning about endangered animals, and that the bald eagle has been endangered. There is a law that says we must protect them."

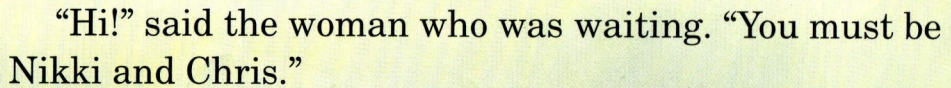

"What do you do to protect them here?" asked Nikki.

"We observe, or watch, them very carefully," said Bess. "We write down everything we learn about them. In this way, we can help eagles that do not live in safe places like refuges. In order to protect the eagle, we must protect the wilderness and all of the animals who live here. All living things depend on each other for survival."

"How many bald eagles are there here?" asked Chris.

"Between forty and fifty this spring," said Bess. "Have you ever seen a bald eagle before?"

"I see them every day," said Nikki.

"No way!" said Chris.

"Yessir! The bald eagle is on every dollar bill!" laughed Nikki.

"That's true," said Bess. "Many years ago, the bald eagle was chosen as the symbol of the United States of America. It was chosen because it is both strong and beautiful, like our country. It can be found on coins and in many other places. The bald eagle is the largest hunting bird in North America."

"Besides here, where do the *real* ones live?" asked Chris.

"Bald eagles live across much of North America. They are fish eagles, so they live near rivers, ponds, and lakes."

"Do they eat other things besides fish?" asked Nikki.

"Bald eagles are birds of prey," said Bess.

"I didn't know birds could pray," said Chris.

"Not that kind of prey," laughed Bess. "Prey are the animals that hunting animals kill and eat. If the bald eagle can't find fish, it will eat rabbits, turtles, squirrels, ducks, and even mice. Sometimes it will eat dead animals if it can't find live ones, and steal prey that other birds have caught

Well, let's get going," said Bess. "We have a lot to see and learn today."

They walked on a trail for a short way.

"I hope there are no wild animals nearby," said Chris, looking from left to right. Nikki laughed at him.

"Yeah, you're so brave just because you went to camp last summer," said Chris.

"Don't worry," said Bess. "The wild animals in these woods are even more afraid of *you*!"

They came to a big river. A small green motorboat was tied to a pole in the water.

"Climb in, kids, and put on these life jackets." Bess put on her life jacket and started the boat.

Chris had never been in a boat before. He held tightly on to the sides.

"We're off!" Bess said.

Chapter 2 — White-Headed Eagles

The green boat came around the bend in the river.

"Did you hear that?" Bess asked the children. "The best way to find eagles is to listen for them. That was a bald eagle's call."

"Is it warning us to stay away?" asked Chris, looking worried.

"No. They're pretty used to me and my boat. But people *can* bother nesting eagles. And if they do, the

eagles may stop nesting."

Bess turned the boat toward the shore.

"Look!" Bess said softly. She pointed to a tall pine tree near the shore. "There are two bald eagles in that big nest!"

"They don't look bald to me," said Chris. "They have white feathers on their heads!"

"You're right, Chris," said Bess. "Bald eagles are not bald. When the English came to North America long ago, they saw the white head of this eagle. They named it the bald eagle. The word *balde* in Old English meant 'white.' So the bald eagle was the white-headed eagle. Both the males and the females have white heads and tail feathers."

"Then how do you tell a boy from a girl?" asked Nikki.

"The female is bigger," said Bess. "Her wingspan can be more than seven feet (2.13 meters). The male's wingspan is about six and one-half feet (1.98 meters)."

"Ha, ha," laughed Nikki. "You boys think you're the only big and strong ones!"

"Just look at the size of that nest, kids. Bald eagle nests can be three to twelve feet (1.09 to 4.36 meters) deep. Some can be ten feet (3.05 meters) wide. That's almost as long as a small car! This nest is about that big, so it must be very old."

"Do they ever build a new nest?" asked Chris.

"Only if something happens to the old one. They just add twigs and branches to the old one each year. The nest is very strong. Even high winds cannot blow it down. To make the nest soft inside, they add leaves, pine needles, moss, and grass. Look over in that other tree. There's another nest. If something happens to the one they're in, they can use that one. I hope those eagles will soon be parents. There are eggs in that nest."

"Wow!" said Nikki. "How many eggs will the female lay?"

"Females lay from one to three eggs. They are white and a little bigger than a chicken's eggs. The pair take turns sitting on them for about thirty-five days, until they hatch. The eggs must be protected from the cold. I hope they have more luck with these eggs," said Bess.

"Did they have bad luck with other eggs?" asked Chris.

"Yes, and they didn't hatch. We don't know why. We *do* know that it was not because of their old problems," said Bess.

"What were their old problems?" asked Nikki.

"Once, there were many bald eagles in North America. They could be found along many big rivers and lakes almost everywhere. Then, about a hundred years ago, hunters shot them in great numbers. Some killed them for sport. Other people killed them because they felt they ate too many fish and killed lambs. But there was enough fish for everyone, and very few lambs were killed by eagles. Still, over 100,000 bald eagles were killed by people."

"That's terrible," said Chris.

"Well, things got even worse for all birds of prey. People started using a poison spray called DDT. It was sprayed on food crops to kill bugs and other pests. Rainwater that ran across the land carried the poison into lakes, rivers, streams, and oceans. Many fish were poisoned. Many birds who ate the fish were poisoned. Some died, and some could not have babies. The poison inside them made their eggshells soft and thin. Many eggs broke before the chicks could be born. The bald eagle was one of the birds with this big problem. Across the land, they and other birds became endangered."

"That means the birds were beginning to die off, and there were very few left," said Nikki.

"That's right." said Bess. "In 1972, a law was made. People were not allowed to use DDT anymore. Soon,

the numbers of bald eagles began to grow. There have been more of them ever since that time."

"Are bald eagles still endangered?" asked Chris.

"In most places in the United States, they are now no longer endangered, except in the Southwest. They are still called threatened, which means we must still be careful to protect them. Did you know that eagles mate for life? That could be twenty-five years or more. Let's hope every eagle will be able to live out its life in as much safety as we can provide. Come on, kids, let's try to find some more eagles!"

Chapter 3: The Hungry Eaglets

Bess steered the boat along the bend of the river. Suddenly, she turned off the motor.

"Look, kids," she said, pointing up toward a tall dead tree.

Perched on a branch hanging over the water was a female bald eagle. Suddenly, she dove down from the tree. As she came near the water, she stretched out her legs. Splash! She hit the water and quickly rose back up. She had caught a large catfish in her hooked talons.

The female eagle flew up to a large nest. She dropped the fish into the nest. The father eagle was perched on the edge of the nest.

"What are those chirping sounds?" said Nikki.

"There are two eaglets in the nest," said Bess. "We have been watching them since they were born, six weeks ago."

"Why are the eaglets bobbing up and down like that?" asked Chris.

"The eaglets are pecking at the fish," said Bess. "The mother is probably trying to teach them to feed themselves. They had both helped to feed them."

The eaglets kept pecking at the fish. They didn't know what else to do. Suddenly, the fish flopped out of the nest! The eaglets jumped back in surprise. They were so afraid that they began to shake. Then one of them looked over the side of the nest as if to say, "What happened to our dinner?" Bess and the children laughed.

The father eagle flew down from the branch. He picked up the fish and brought it back to the nest. This time, he and the mother eagle tore up the fish for the eaglets.

"I guess they will have to learn to feed themselves another day!" said Nikki.

After eating, the eaglets jumped and played in the big nest. One of them tossed a stick into the air!

Bess explained that the eaglets had lost their first baby-soft feathers, or down. Now their down was thicker, like a warm coat. Their first brownish black feathers were starting to grow.

The father eagle flew from the nest.

"It's the father's turn to hunt," said Bess. "The eaglets are always hungry. They have to be fed many times a day. The mother and father also have to hunt

for themselves. Each of them eats four to five fish a day or whatever else it can find."

The father eagle rose in spirals, or circles, in the sky. Soon he was soaring high. He didn't need to flap his long, wide wings. The rising air carried him.

Bess started the boat again and headed toward a wider part of the river. The wind began to pick up a bit, so Bess steered closer to the shore. The boat rocked in the waves.

"I think I feel seasick," said Chris.

"Don't you mean 'riversick'?" laughed Nikki.

The wind blew harder. Water splashed into the boat. The children gripped its sides. Even Nikki looked scared.

"I'm heading toward shore," Bess shouted over the sound of the wind. "The river can get very rough!"

As they came close to the shore, the small boat hit something with a loud thud.

"Oh no," said Bess, turning off the motor. "We're stuck between two rocks that are just below the water. We'll have to try to push away from them."

"I'm in the front," said Chris. "I can help."

"Great!" said Bess. "It's too rough for me to stand up. Chris, when I start the motor, you try to push us away from rocks with this oar."

Bess started the motor. Chris pushed as hard as he

could with the oar. He pushed and pushed. After a few tries, the boat was freed from the rocks!

"Good work, Chris!" said Bess.

"Thanks!" said Chris, looking quite proud.

"We're lucky. We're very close to where we were going," said Bess. She headed the boat to a small sandy shore. She jumped out of the boat and pulled it onto the sand.

"Let's go," said Bess. "Are you ready for *more* adventures?"

"As long as they're on land!" Chris said.

Chapter 4   Flying Lessons

"Nikki and Chris, we're near another place to observe eagles," said Bess. Bess reached under her seat and brought out a large, long bag. "We'll use this spotting scope to see things that are far away. Follow me!"

Bess led the way down a narrow trail.

"Isn't this great?" Nikki asked Chris. "I love being away from the noisy city. Everything is beautiful here." She took a deep breath. "It even *smells* great here."

"I've never smelled so much fresh air," said Chris. "It *is* awesome. I guess you were right, Nikki. There's a lot to learn about here."

"Where are we going?" Nikki asked Bess.

"Just up ahead," said Bess. They climbed up a hill right by the trail.

"This is one of our lookout spots. I will point the scope toward a tree that has another bald eagle nest. There are two six-week-old eaglets in the nest." She set up the scope and focused it.

"Look how well you can see the nest, even though it's far away," Bess said.

Nikki looked first. "Wow! I can see an eagle on the nest. I can even see its yellow beak. It looks so sharp! But I don't see any eaglets. How do you know there are eaglets there, Bess?"

"We've been watching this nest for many weeks

now," Bess answered. "Helpers called volunteers give their time to help us watch and get information."

Chris looked through the scope next.

"It's like I'm right next to the eagle! How big are the eaglets?" he asked.

"They probably weigh about eight or nine pounds now," said Bess. "They grow very quickly. Soon, they will be about as big as their parents. At about four months old, bald eagles are almost full grown."

"When will they learn how to fly?" asked Chris.

"They fledge, or learn how to fly, at about ten to twelve weeks old," said Bess. "At first, they just practice. They hop and jump above the nest."

"Then do they fly away?" asked Chris.

"No, Chris. Learning how to fly is not that easy for young bald eagles. They are so big and their wings are so long that they often have trouble at first. They can be funny to watch when they first leave the nest. They often crash into trees and bushes because they don't know how to land!"

The children laughed.

"The parents often feed the eaglets for a while after fledgling," said Bess. "It takes time for the eaglets to learn how to hunt well. They may stay close to their nest for six to twelve weeks or even longer. When they begin to hunt, they often feed on dead animals or whatever is easy to catch."

Bess was interrupted by a "kweek kuk kuk, kweek-akuk-kuk."

"What's that?" asked Nikki.

"Look! Up in that tree. It's another bald eagle!" said Chris.

"That's not a very loud sound for such a big bird," said Nikki.

"You're right," said Bess. "Some much smaller birds make a lot more noise! Eagle sounds are often high and squeaky."

The eagle in the nest perched on it and then flew off.

"It's the father's turn to hunt again," said Bess. "It's not easy being a bald eagle parent."

Chapter 5 — Soaring High

They watched the male fly high into the sky.

"I wish I could soar like that," said Nikki. "I would feel so free! How fast and how far can they fly, Bess?"

"They may dive through the air at a hundred miles per hour! Bald eagles may fly hundreds of miles a day when they are migrating. Some birds and other animals migrate, or travel to other places, before the winter. They migrate to find food or mates. Eagles try to save energy by not flapping so much. They can go farther by soaring and gliding. They use the thermals to do this."

"I have thermal underwear," laughed Chris. They all laughed.

"Well, thermals *do* have something to do with heat," said Bess. "When the sun heats the land and water, the air currents rise up. Eagles soar with these warm currents, or thermals. They hardly beat their wings. They can circle hundreds of feet into the air."

Bess said, "He might fly for many miles searching for any sign of food."

Suddenly, they heard a call: "Kwick, kwick." They looked up and saw two young eagles. They were mostly brown and had some white feathers on their bellies. They circled around one another. Then they locked their talons together and tumbled with one another in the air. They cartwheeled toward the water. All at once, they let go of one another. Then they both flapped hard until they flew away high into the sky.

"Wow!" Nikki and Chris said at the same time.

Bess explained, "Those young eagles were playing! Bald eagles will also do this when they are mating, but these eagles are too young to mate."

"Look up!" said Bess. "The father eagle is still soaring in and out of those clouds." Suddenly, he dove through the air at a great speed, landed in a field, and rose back up again.

"Now he's on that branch!" Chris nearly shouted. "He has a rabbit. Bess, how could he see it from so far up?"

"Eagles have very sharp eyes," Bess answered. "They can see about a mile away. Also, their claws and talons are two inches (5.08 centimeters) long to grab and carry heavy prey. After he eats, he will probably hunt for the eaglets. The wind has died down. We'd better start to head back."

"Oh no! It seems like we just got here," said Chris.
"I *knew* you'd love it here!" said Nikki.
"Well, I hope you'll come back to the refuge again soon, to find out how the eaglets are doing!" said Bess.

Chapter 6 — Free Again!

They walked back down the trail.

"You know," said Bess, "the North American Indians loved all of the eagles. Eagles were honored for their beauty, strength, and courage. The Indians told many tales about eagles. One legend said that the bald eagle was the only bird who could fly to the sun. In the legend, the eagle pushed the sun across the sky. Then the sun's great heat turned the eagle's head and tail feathers

white. Also, when an Indian fought well in battle, he could wear eagle feathers in his hair. This meant he was strong and brave."

"Before this, I never thought much about *real* bald eagles," said Chris.

"Many people don't," said Bess. "In the past, they may not have known that eagles were endangered. Some knew but didn't care. Many of those who did care worked to save the eagle. We now know that birds of prey are important predators. Do you know what predators are?"

"We learned that, too," said Nikki. "A predator is an animal that hunts and kills other animals for food. Our teacher said we need predators to keep the balance in nature. If this didn't happen, there would be too many of one kind of animal and not enough of another."

"Yes," said Bess, "and without balance, nature doesn't work well. Many eagles still die because of what people have done or made. Some are shot. Some are killed when they perch on power lines that are 'live,' which means in use. Some are killed by cars or get tangled in fishing lines."

"And we build highways and buildings in wild places. Then there may not be enough places for them to live, hunt, and build nests," said Chris.

"And they may become sick from polluted water and food," said Nikki.

"How can people help?" asked Chris.

"We can do a lot of things," said Bess. "We can protect nest trees. We can make laws so that people will not fish in eagle breeding places. We can make more and bigger wildlife refuges like this one so the eagle and other animals can live in peace and safety."

"Can kids help, too?" asked Chris.

"You bet," said Bess. "Tell others why all animals must be protected. When you are older, you can even volunteer at a refuge near your home."

"And everyone should help keep the earth clean by not littering," said Nikki.

"That's right!" said Bess. "Caring about the earth is the first step toward saving it. Let everyone know that we are making the bald eagle free again!"

"We will!" they both said.

"And we'll be back here, soon!" said Chris.

"I *told* you," laughed Nikki.

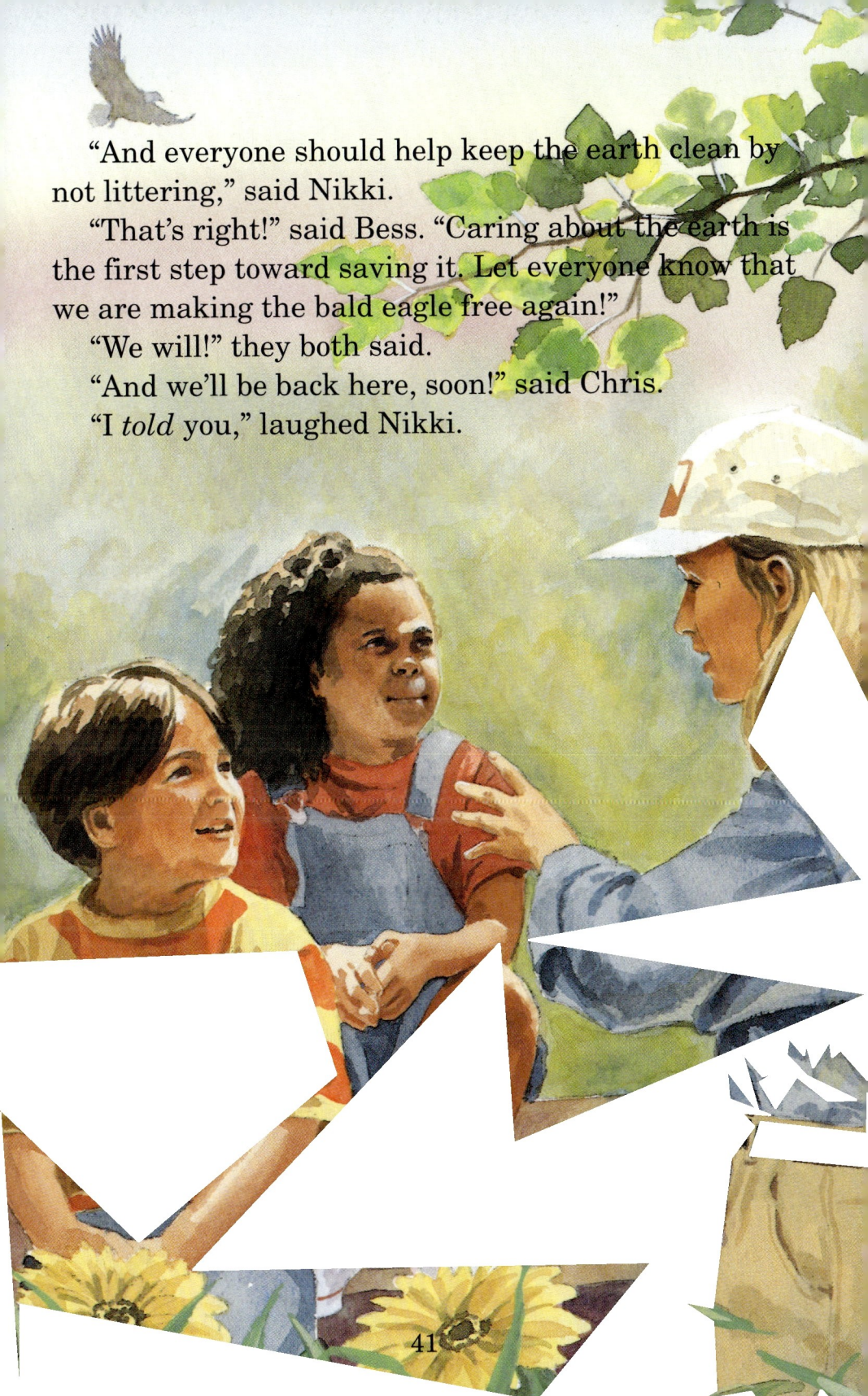

Glossary

beak The adult bald eagle's nose, or beak, is yellow and about two inches (5 centimeters) long. It is very sharp and is used for tearing apart its prey.

birds of prey Birds of prey kill and eat animals for food. Some birds of prey include eagles, hawks, and owls. Birds of prey are also called raptors (RAP-tors).

breed A living thing must breed, or mate, in order to make more of its own kind. Each creature has its own breeding season, or time of the year in which it mates.

eaglet (EAG-let) An eaglet is a young eagle. Bald eagle eaglets weigh about two ounces (57 grams) when they are born. They grow very fast. At one month they weigh more than seven pounds (3.2 kilos). Their first adult feathers start to grow.

egg The egg of a bird is produced by the female and contains the young bird. After laying one or more eggs, the mother bird (and often the father) keep them warm so they will hatch. The young birds grow inside the eggs.

endangered (en-DAN-gered) An animal or plant becomes endangered when there are not many of its kind left in the world.

feathers (FEA-thers) Feathers make up the protective body covering of birds. A bird uses its feathers for many reasons. When the sun is hot, feathers shade the eagle's skin and protect it. In cold weather, feathers keep the eagle warm. The eagle grows a new coat of feathers every year.

fish eagle The bald eagle is called a fish eagle because it eats mostly fish; however, it will also eat many other things.

immature (imm-a-TURE) The word immature means "young" or "not adult." Young bald eagles are immature until they are about four to five years old.

legend (LEG-end) A legend is a story that has been handed down from the long-ago past.

mate Animals must find a partner, or mate, in order to have babies. Bald eagles usually mate for life. If something happens to their mate, they will find another mate. Eagles look for mates during the breeding season.

migration (mi-GRA-tion) When the seasons change, some animals migrate, or move from one place to another. When bald eagles migrate, they may travel 200 miles a day without a rest.

Old English (Old ENG-lish) The people from England are called English. Many years ago, they spoke a language called Old English. When some of the English came to settle in North America, they spoke Old English.

pollute (poll-UTE) To pollute something is to make it unclean and unsafe. The earth, water, and air can become polluted when harmful things are put there. People, animals, and plants can become sick and even die from some kinds of pollution.

power lines (POW-er lines) Power lines carry electricity to buildings. If a bird perches on a power line or wire that is being used, it can become badly shocked and even die.

predator (PRED-a-tor) A predator is an animal that hunts and kills other animals for food.

prey Prey is an animal that is hunted by another animal for food.

thermal (THER-mal) A thermal is a rising current of warm air. A bird riding a thermal may soar up to 14,000 feet (4300 meters).

threatened When we speak of a "threatened" animal, we mean one that is likely to become endangered if it is not protected. At this time, there are about 200 plants and animals listed as threatened in the United States.

wildlife biologist (WILD-life bi-OL-o-gist) A wildlife biologist is trained in the science of plants and animals. He or she studies how animals live and behave. On a wildlife refuge, the wildlife biologist must work to ensure that there is enough space, food, and protection for all of the animals living there. The information wildlife biologists learn also helps to protect animals not in refuges.

wildlife refuge (WILD-life REF-uge) A wildlife refuge is a place where wildlife and their habitats (places to live) are protected. There are more than 450 wildlife refuges in the United States.

Dear Parents and Educators:

Welcome to the Young Readers' series!

These learning stories have been created to introduce young children to the study of animals.

Children's earliest exposure to reading is usually through fiction. Stories read aloud invite children into the world of words and imagination. If children are read to frequently, this becomes a highly anticipated form of entertainment. Often that same pleasure is felt when children learn to read on their own. Nonfiction books are also read aloud to children but generally when they are older. However, interest in the "real" world emerges early in life, as soon as children develop a sense of wonder about everything around them.

There are a number of excellent read-aloud natural-science books available. Educators and parents agree that children love nonfiction books about animals. Unfortunately, there are very few that can be read *by* young children. One of the goals of the Young Readers' series is to happily fill that gap!

The Bald Eagle is one in a series of learning stories designed to appeal to young readers. In the classroom, the series can be incorporated into literature-based or whole-language programs, and would be especially suitable for science theme teaching units. Within planned units, each book may serve as a springboard to immersion techniques that include hands-on activities, field study trips, and additional research and reading. Many of the books are also concerned with the threatened or endangered status of the species studied and the role even young people can play in the preservation plan.

These books can also serve as read-aloud for young children. Weaving information through a story form lends itself easily to reading aloud. Hopefully, this book and others in the series will provide entertainment and wonder for both young readers and listeners.

C.A.

Guidelines for the Young Readers' Series

In the Classroom

One of the goals of this series is to introduce the young child to factual information related to the species being studied. The science terminology used is relevant to the learning process for the young student. In the classroom, you may want to use multi-modality methods to ensure understanding and word recognition. The following suggestions may be helpful:

1. Refer to the pictures when possible for difficult words and discuss how these words can be used in another context.
2. Encourage the children to use word and sentence contextual clues when approaching unknown words. They should be encouraged to use the glossary since it is an important information adjunct to the story.
3. After the children read the story or individual chapter, you may want to involve them in discussions using a variety of questioning techniques:

    a. Questions requiring *recall* ask the children about past experiences, observations, or feelings. (*Have you ever seen movies or TV programs about bald eagles?*)

    b. *Process* questions help the children to discover relationships by asking them to compare, classify, infer, or explain. (*Do you have to eat every day? Does the bald eagle? Why or why not?*)

    c. *Application* questions ask children to use new information in a hypothetical situation by evaluating, imagining, or predicting.

At Home

The above aids can be used if your child is reading independently or aloud. Children will also enjoy hearing this story read aloud to them. You may want to use some of the questioning suggestions above. The story may provoke many questions from your child. Stop and answer the questions. Replying with an honest, "I don't know," provides a wonderful opportunity to head for the library to do some research together!

Have a wonderful time in your shared quest of discovery learning!

    Carol A. Amato
    Language-Learning Specialist